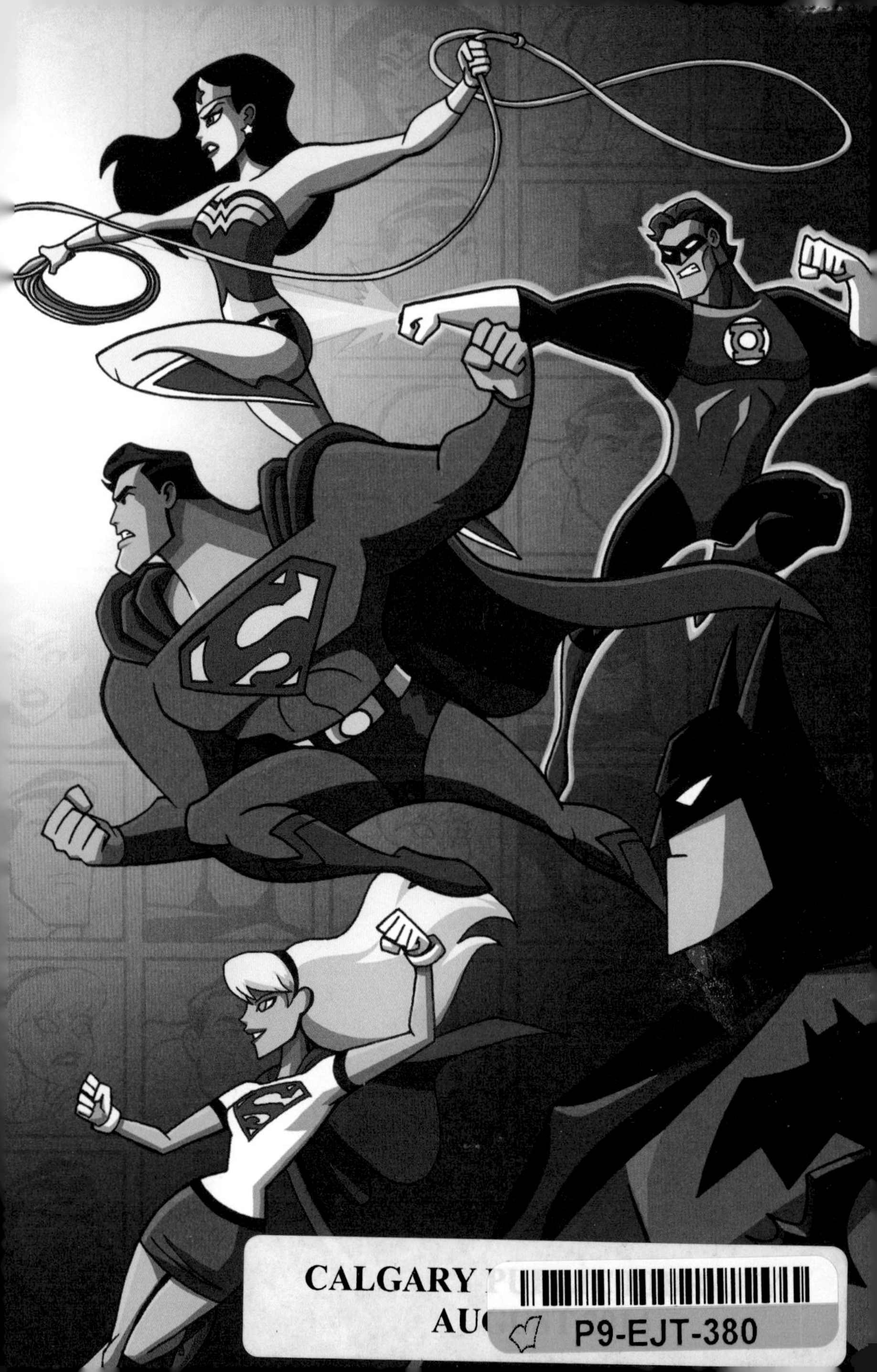

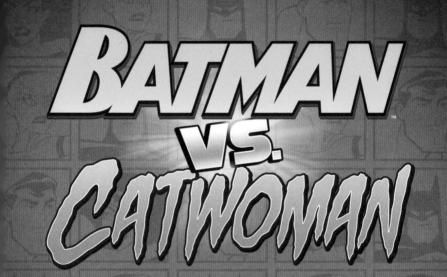

BATMAN VS. CATWOMAN

WRITTEN BY
J.E. BRIGHT

ILLUSTRATED BY
TIM LEVINS

COVER ILLUSTRATION BY
LUCIANO VECCHIO

BATMAN CREATED BY
BOB KANE

STONE ARCH BOOKS
a capstone imprint

Published by Stone Arch Books in 2013
A Capstone Imprint
1710 Roe Crest Drive
North Mankato, MN 56003
www.capstonepub.com

Cataloging-in-Publication Data is available at the Library
of Congress website
ISBN: 978-1-4342-6013-0 (library binding)

Summary: When a priceless, jewel-encrusted bird statue
is installed atop a skyscraper in Gotham, Catwoman
has her eyes--and her claws--on the prize. But when she
puts her paws on the curious statue, this feline gets
caught up in the Penguin's fowl power play...

Designed by Hilary Wacholz

Printed in the United States of America in Stevens Point, Wisconsin.
032013   007227WZF13

TABLE OF CONTENTS

CHAPTER 1
COBBLEPOT TOWER................................... 6

CHAPTER 2
CATS, BIRDS, AND BATS............................. 14

CHAPTER 3
HIGHRISE ACROBATICS............................... 21

CHAPTER 4
BATTY BIRDS....................................... 29

CHAPTER 5
FOR THE BIRDS..................................... 38

BATMAN™

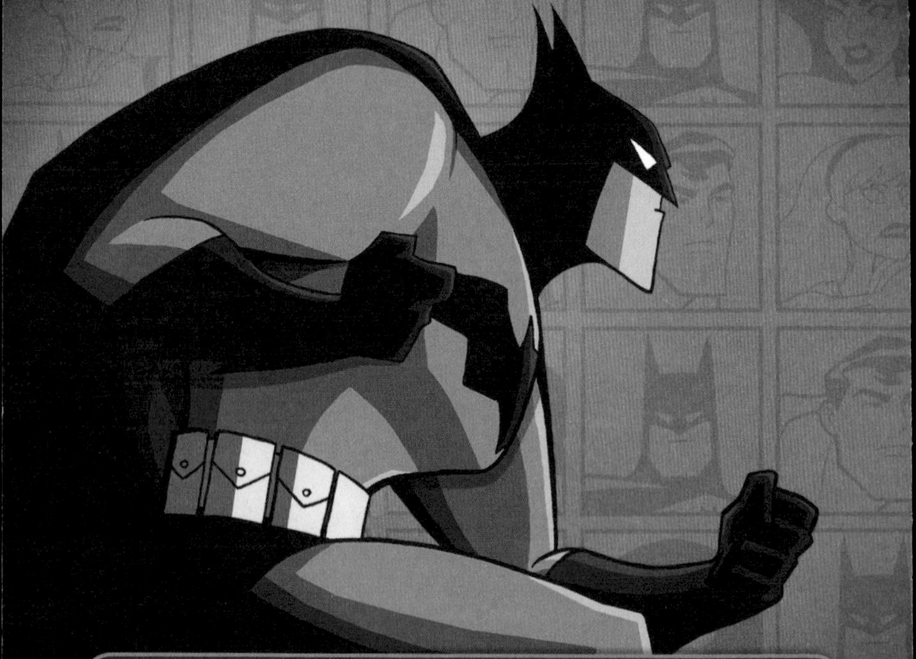

REAL NAME: Bruce Wayne

ROLE: Crime fighter

BASE: The Batcave in Gotham City

ABILITIES: The Dark Knight is a master detective. His talent in martial arts is without equal. He has access to a variety of useful gadgets and weaponry via the Utility Belt he wears around his waist.

CATWOMAN

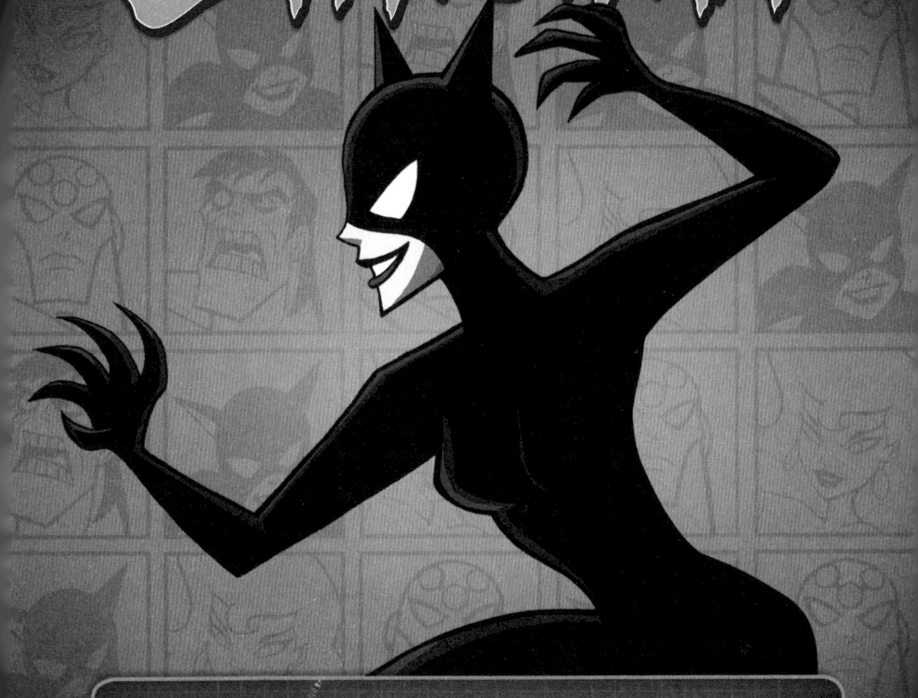

REAL NAME: Selina Kyle

ROLE: Professional criminal

BASE: Gotham City's criminal underworld

ABILITIES: Catwoman is a master thief. She is as agile as a gymnast, stealthy as a cat, and an excellent hand-to-hand combatant. She has a soft spot for cats and orphans.

CHAPTER 1

COBBLEPOT TOWER

Selina Kyle pushed herself into the shadowed side of an exposed steel I-beam. A security guard who was doing his rounds in the partially-built building walked into view a moment later. The guard shined his flashlight along the unfinished construction on the dark top floor of Cobblepot Tower.

She saw a tangle of exposed wires in the walls. PVC pipes twisted across the ceiling. Stacks of drywall boards and white buckets of plaster were on the raw concrete floor. They glowed eerily in the flashlight's swinging beam.

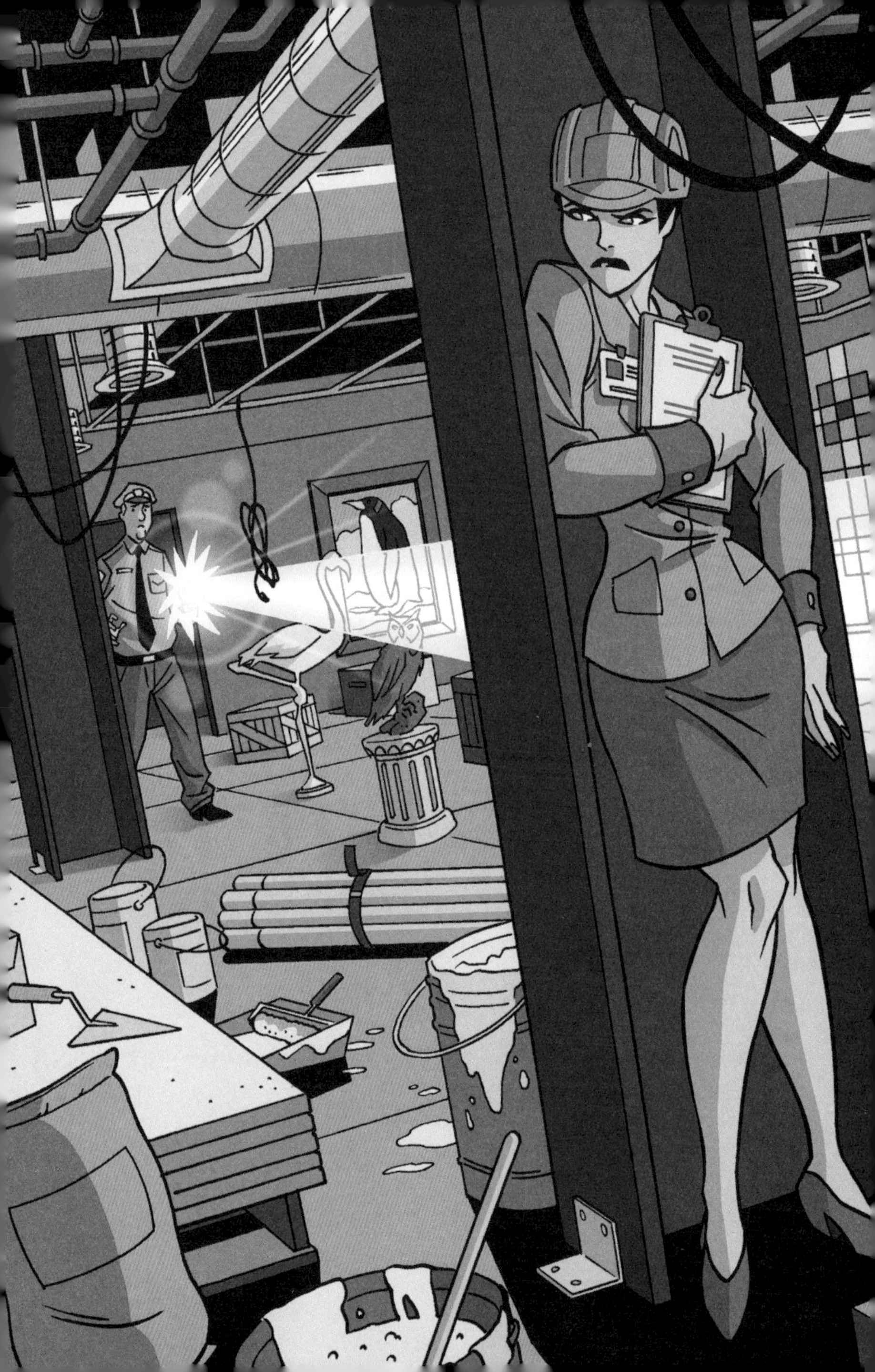

Even if the security guard spotted Selina, she looked the part. She wore a sensible women's business suit and a hardhat. She also carried a clipboard and had an official-looking badge clipped to her lapel. She was ready to act like an overworked inspector who was doing a late-night check on the construction to make sure it was up to code. In Selina's experience, looking the part was almost always enough. And if absolutely necessary, Selina could simply knock out the guard.

Selina had easily snuck past the guards on the ground floor. She took the construction elevator in the back of the building, which she knew wasn't hooked up to the security system. Now she was in a room that was soon to be Oswald Cobblepot's office.

Marble wall panels and statues of all kinds of birds rested at various angles around the room. On one wall was a huge painting of a penguin.

The Penguin is such a birdbrain, thought Catwoman. Although she had to admit that he'd become impressively rich ever since his Iceberg Lounge had become popular. To show off the Penguin's newfound wealth, Cobblepot Tower was built. It was quite a sight — even in its unfinished state.

Finally, the guard finished his inspection of the office. He whistled as he moved on, heading down a corridor of exposed metal framework toward the executive dining room area. He disappeared down a hall.

As soon as the guard was out of earshot, Selina stepped out of the I-beam's shadow.

She slunk across the office toward a sturdy door. This door was made of steel, with a high-tech lock on it along with an eye scanner. Only a thin sheet of taped plastic covered the steel hinges that connected the door to the wall.

After peeling back the plastic sheet just enough to access the bolts in the hinges, Selina slid a slim power screwdriver out from her wig. She quickly unscrewed the eight bolts in the two hinges, popping them out into her hand. When she removed the last bolt, Selina pulled firmly on the top hinge.

CRRREEEEEAK! The door slid out of its frame, tilting forward. It hit the floor with a solid **THUD!**

Because the door remained connected to its lock, the alarm didn't sound.

There was only a narrow space between the door and the doorway that Selina easily squeezed through.

Selina pulled off the wig and hardhat, then shuffled out of her business outfit. She stood in the atrium at the base of a spiral staircase in her real clothes — a black catsuit with a mask that had sleek and pointed ears. In this outfit, Selina felt most comfortable. It was who she truly was, really.

She was Catwoman.

She quickly climbed the twisting staircase that threaded upward to the top of the tower. After climbing a few flights, Catwoman reached a platform, a little room that was just barely tall enough for her to stand inside.

On the northern side of the sky-high room was an iron door that looked like a hatch to a submarine. Catwoman twirled the wheel once, then twice, and then pushed the door open.

WOOOOOOOOSH!

As she stuck her head outside into the open sky, wind whipped past the doorway, tugging at her mask. Along the outside of the high capsule was a sort of iron ladder attached to the curved metal wall.

She stepped onto the lowest rung of the ladder, holding onto the doorway and a higher rung. Gotham spread out below her in a dizzying panorama.

"Good thing I'm not afraid of heights," Catwoman said to herself. She began to climb.

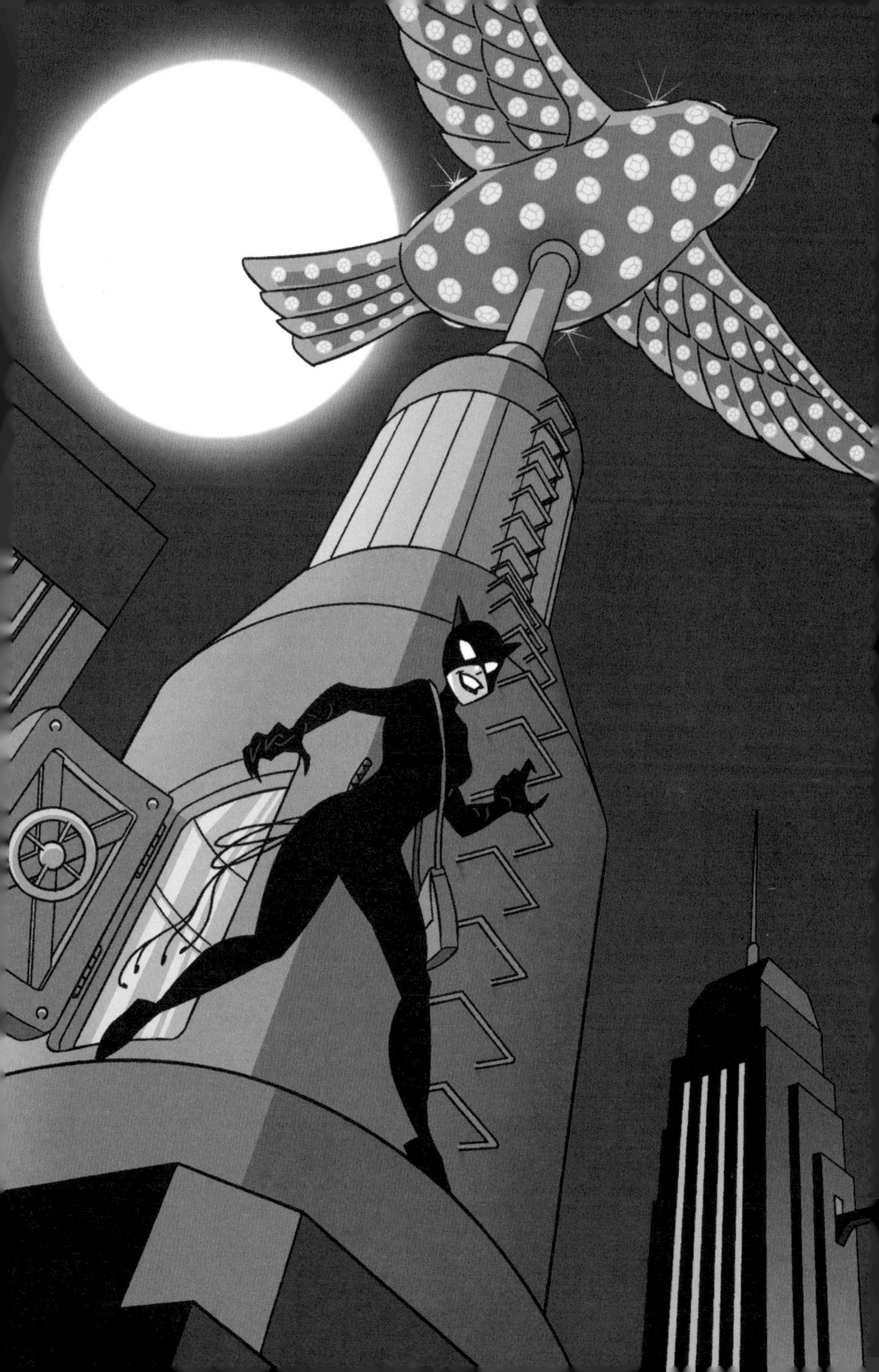

CHAPTER 2

CATS, BIRDS, AND BATS

Halfway up the ladder of iron rungs, Catwoman took a second to absorb the breathtaking view of Gotham City at night.

It was a twisted metropolis filled with shadows. Like a graveyard. The tower lights glowing in Gotham's skyline went nicely with the gloomy clouds above. Below, the grubby harbor swayed on the river's black bank, and the red and white lights of the dense traffic on the highway pulsed like a living organism. Gotham was dangerous, difficult, and filled with corruption.

Catwoman smiled. *There's no place like home,* she thought.

She continued the single-story climb up the rungs. She stopped just under an unusual statue at the top. It was only a little smaller than a compact car, and was shaped like a giant sparrow in flight.

Most importantly, it was studded all over with huge industrial diamonds. Catwoman simply could not resist snatching some of those big beautiful jewels. They had been set into the sparrow so that spotlights would make it glow over the city like a giant disco ball. It would be quite a sight, but Catwoman thought that the diamonds would look even lovelier in her hidden bank vault. That is, until she sold them on the black market and made a very tidy profit.

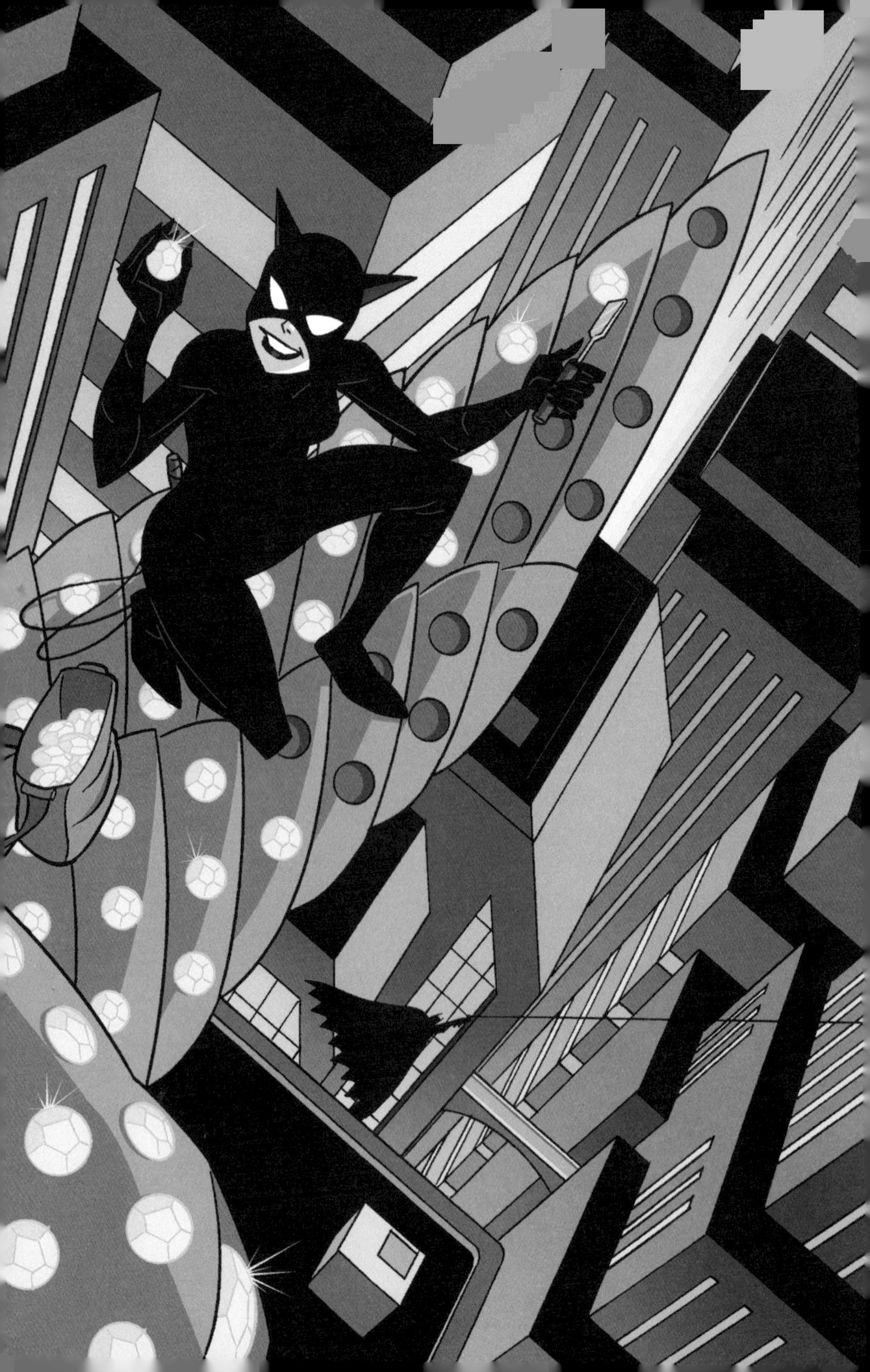

Catwoman scrambled onto the platform that held the jeweled bird. She hoisted herself up so she was sitting on top of one of the sparrow's outstretched wings. She pulled a small chisel out of her belt.

CLANK! She pried a diamond out of the statue's shiny metal feathers. **PLUNK.** She dropped it into a satin bag, then started chiseling at the next one.

As she worked, she started to grow nervous. Getting up to the jeweled bird had been easy. Too easy. Catwoman peered around at the lower towers nearby, checking for potential threats.

The teetering tower crane that had been used to install the sparrow statue that morning was still looming alongside the building, attached to the corner.

Catwoman had considered using the crane to reach the statue, but she would have been too visible against the night sky. Half the city could have seen her.

Catwoman leaned in close to the biggest diamonds in the eyes. As she peered into one eye, she noticed that it was moving. In fact, it wasn't even a diamond at all. She was surprised to see some sort of gadget inside the curved glass eye — a lens.

Hmm, Catwoman thought, peering into the object. *The lens looks like a projector, or some kind of weapon —*

"Stop!" a deep, amplified voice boomed from the darkness. "Those diamonds do not belong to you."

Catwoman glanced upward to see Batman soaring toward her on a zip line connected to his grapnel gun.

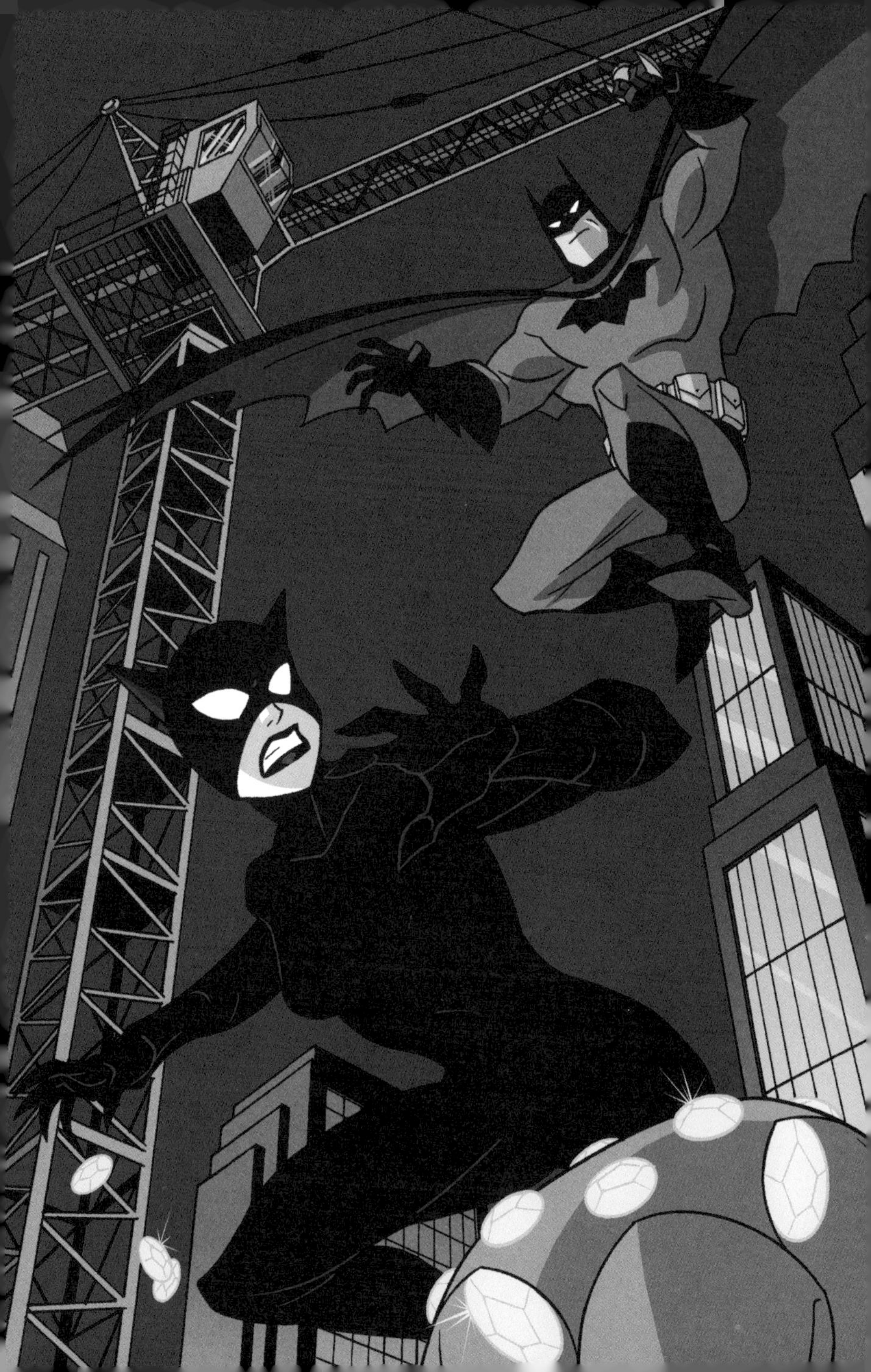

Batman grinned as he hung in the air next to Catwoman. "It looks like I've caught you with your claws in the canary cage," he said.

"Oh, Batman," said Catwoman, both pleased and annoyed to see her most worthy adversary. "You haven't caught me yet."

CHAPTER 3

HIGHRISE ACROBATICS

Before Batman could grab her, Catwoman rolled forward over the head of the bird and pushed herself off Cobblepot Tower. She tucked and somersaulted in the air, unhitching her bullwhip from her belt at the same time.

THUMP! Catwoman landed a quick kick to the side of Batman's head. Then she grabbed hold of his zip line and hung on with her feet.

Batman struggled to hold on. "You're going to get us both killed," he growled.

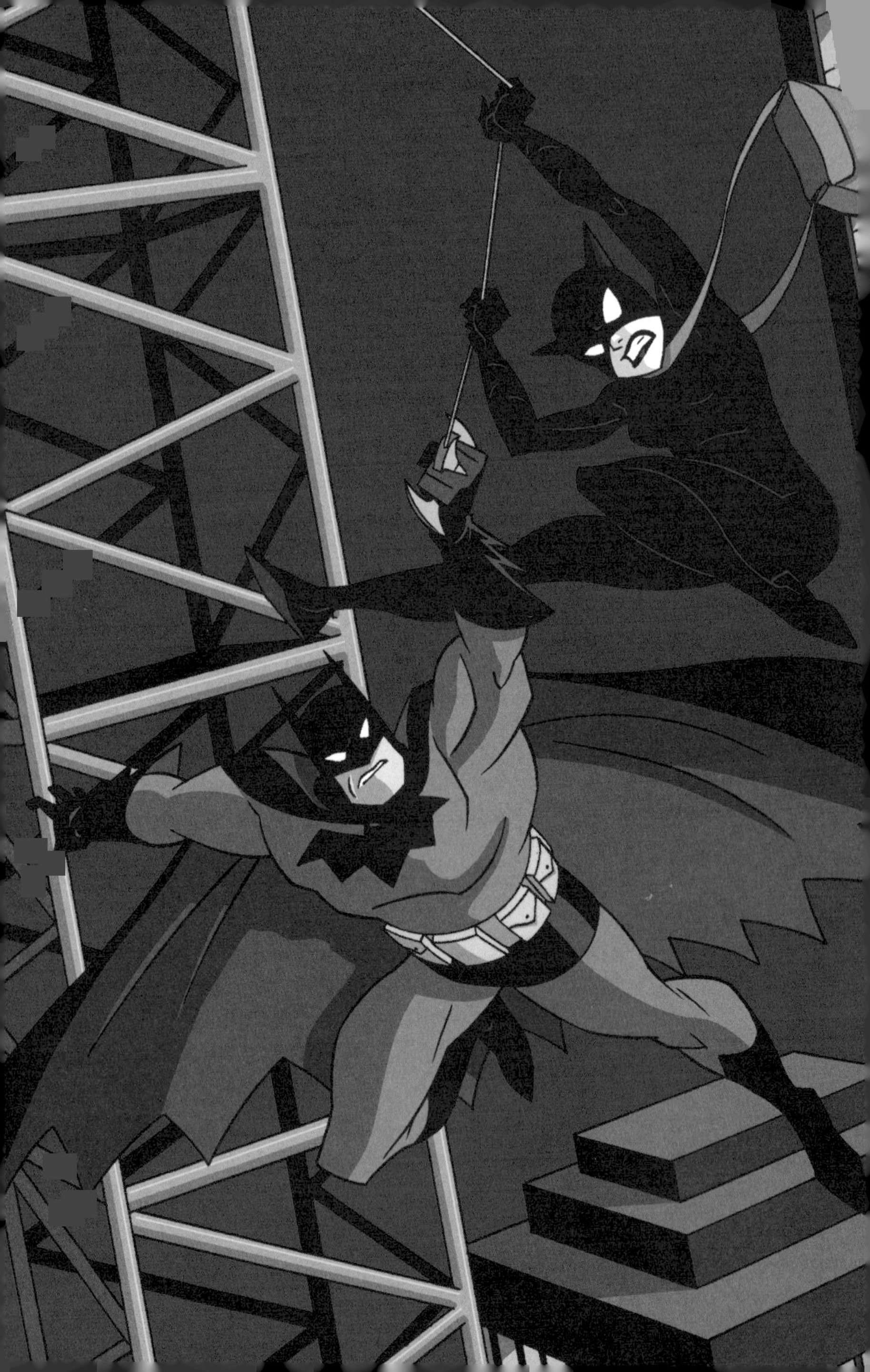

Batman wrapped the rope around his fist to strengthen his grip. Catwoman released the rope then flung out her left heel. She put all her weight behind it, aiming directly at the Dark Knight.

Batman acrobatically swung himself upward. Catwoman ducked, anticipating Batman trying to grab her. The rope swung to the side, but Batman and Catwoman were both able to grab hold. Catwoman hopped off the rope and onto the edge of the building. When Batman tried to do the same, Catwoman kicked at him, knocking him backward.

"You're full of energy tonight," said Batman, glaring at her. "You know I can't let you steal that statue, or its gems."

"I wasn't asking your permission," replied Catwoman.

"Though I must say," Catwoman added, "I'm impressed with your sense of balance."

"Thank you," said Batman. "Unlike you, I'm always on the level."

"Very clever," Catwoman purred. "You've always been good with words."

Suddenly, Catwoman sprang up and cracked her whip. **KA-RACK!** As she expected, it made Batman duck. She leapt to the rungs of the ladder, continuing to snap her whip at Batman to keep him at a distance as she descended. The second she was close enough to the crane's horizontal arm, she snapped her bullwhip upward. **FA-WHIP!** It wrapped around a steel crossbar.

"Sorry to rush away," Catwoman said with a grin.

Batman poised himself, ready to leap after her. But just as he pounced, Catwoman dropped off the crane, swinging on her whip, circling around the tower crane's body.

Batman leaped down, following as fast as he could. Cobblepot Tower didn't give Catwoman much room to swing from while she tried to escape. Batman could see her wherever she jumped. She would have to distract him to get away.

With a flick of her wrist, Catwoman unhooked the tip of her whip from the crane's crossbar. She felt a sharp stab of fear as she hurtled through open space, but then she cracked her whip.

SNAP! It caught a metal rung of the crane's ladder.

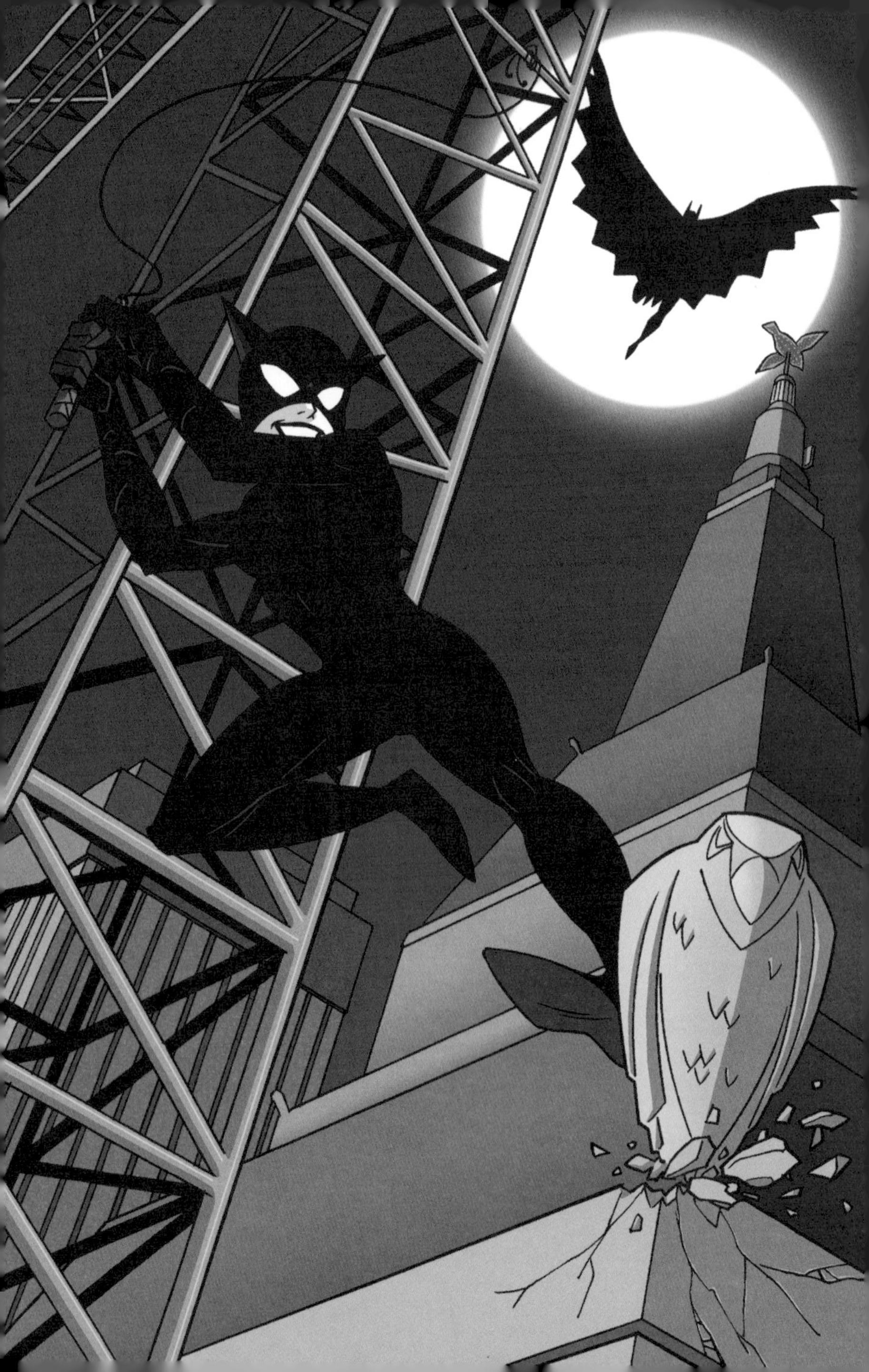

As she whirled around, Catwoman aimed her feet at the small eagle gargoyle on the building's corner. She snapped her whip off the rung, and let herself smash into the eagle feet-first. **KA-THUD!**

The stone statue wobbled as Catwoman landed next to it. As Batman jumped down toward her. **CRUNCH!** It broke free and toppled off the roof corner. Batman watched in horror as it fell toward the city streets below, which were filled with people even at night.

It was an obvious trick, but one that Batman couldn't ignore. If that statue hit the ground, it would likely injure or kill several citizens. Batman glared at Catwoman, then he pulled out his grapnel gun and dived into the air after the plummeting statue.

While Batman was busy, Catwoman hurried across the roof and slipped inside the air vent of an unfinished elevator shaft. She slid down to a service tunnel and ducked into the small space, hiding in the shadows. Batman would assume she'd left Cobblepot Tower, so she didn't actually need to escape. She just needed to wait until he went away.

So Catwoman settled in, curling up comfortably and began playing a silent game on her smartphone to pass the time.

CHAPTER 4

BATTY BIRDS

After a few hours of waiting, Catwoman cautiously climbed up the vent shaft and checked to see if it was safe to leave. When she popped her head out, she heard voices coming from above, near the statue.

Then she heard the familiar, annoying laugh of the Penguin.

Curious, Catwoman slunk across the roof, staying out of sight behind a huge industrial air conditioning unit. If she leaned slightly over the edge of the roof, she could just glimpse the sparrow statue above.

The Penguin sat astride the jeweled statue, cackling. His stumpy legs stuck out awkwardly in either direction. He held a black umbrella that had glowing buttons along its slim shaft.

Below him, gripping a metal rung with one hand, was one of the Penguin's henchmen. The thug was dressed in a white lab coat like a scientist. In his other hand, the man held a long pole with a cage at the end of it. The statue's eyes glistened in the moonlight.

Catwoman focused on the cage. She could see a white pigeon inside, bobbing its head nervously.

"Now!" Penguin ordered his henchman. "I'm ready! Do it now!"

"Initiating test one," the thug stated.

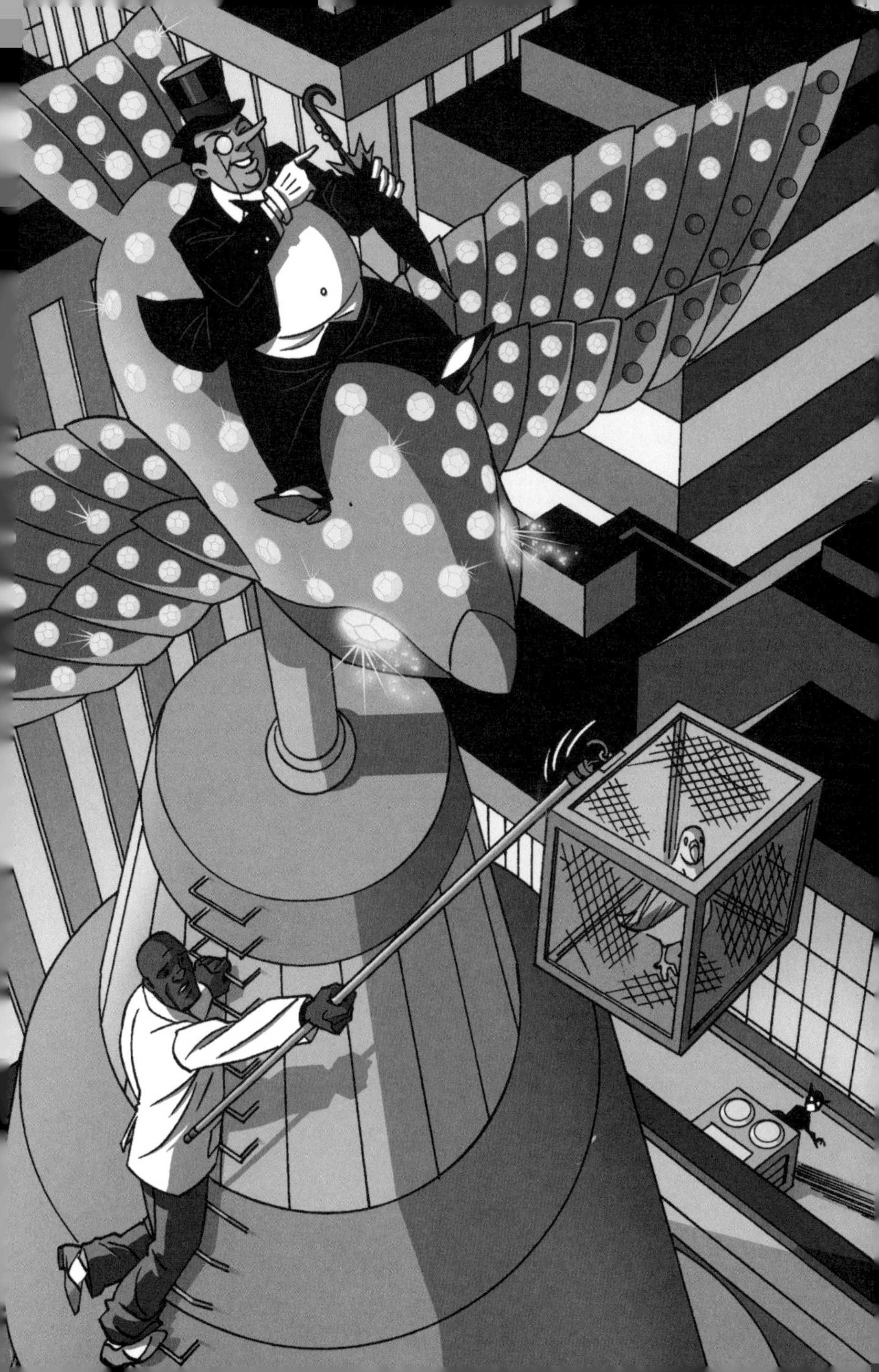

The man extended the pole out in front of the beak of the jeweled sparrow. He held the cage level with the statue's eyes. "Test subject in place. The subject, an ordinary pigeon, seems calm."

"Faster!" Penguin croaked. "Enough of your scientific dilly-dallying!" He pointed his umbrella at the sparrow's head.

CLICK! He pressed a button on its handle. The statue's eyes lit up with blue light. The light grew brighter and brighter until it seemed to be completely white.

Catwoman suspected that the light was still increasing in brightness. She slipped on a pair of slim goggles that let her see ultraviolet light. The goggles also allowed her to see in the dark. Immediately, she saw the sparrow statue's eyes blazing with brilliant ultraviolet light.

The light appeared to glow ever more brightly through her goggles. There was something wrong with the light, though. It looked . . . creepy.

The pigeon inside the cage warbled a strange coo. It stretched out its pudgy body as if it were flexing its muscles.

"REEEEEEEEEEEE!" Catwoman flinched as the pigeon cried out. She'd never heard an animal make a sound like that before. It was a confident sounding call.

It's a war cry, Catwoman realized.

The pigeon rushed to the front of the cage. **PECK! PECK! PECK!** It attacked the wire mesh with its beak. Then it started scraping at the mesh with its claws. Some of the wires were torn in its furious frenzy.

When the pigeon scratched a hole big enough for its head, it began pushing its way out of the cage. The pigeon stretched the mesh with its wriggling body. It was the most aggressive bird Catwoman had ever seen.

Popping out of the cage, the pigeon landed on the pole holding it. The aggressive bird screeched and flapped its wings. It bobbed its head once, and then dived at the scientist henchman holding the pole. The pigeon flapped into the scientist's face, pecking at his head with his beak and scraping with its claws.

The scientist dropped the cage pole so he could protect his head from the vicious pigeon. "Help me!" the thug cried out.

"HAHAHAHAHAHAHA!" The Penguin cackled loudly.

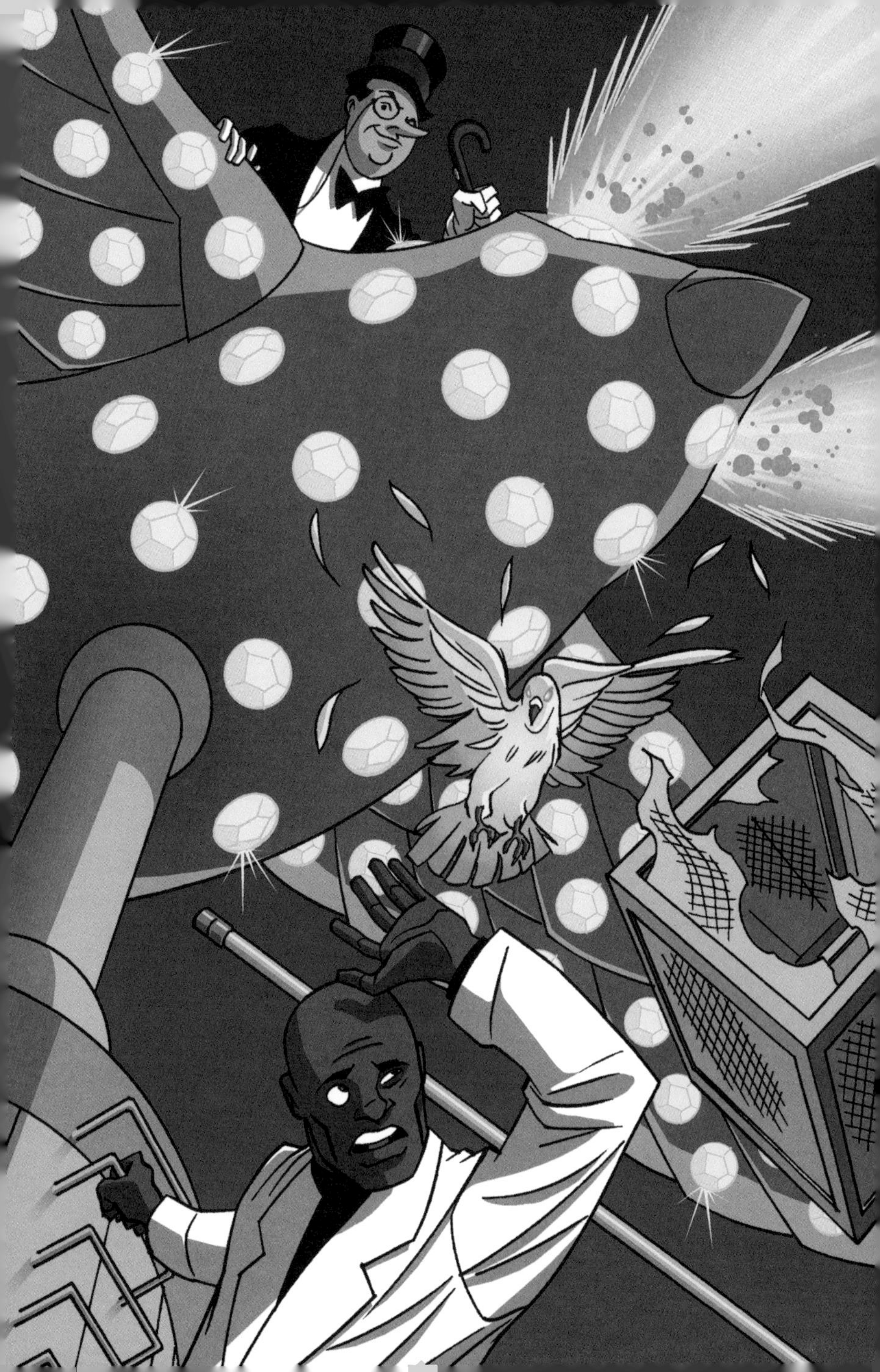

"It works!" the Penguin cheered. "The light makes the birds better! With this, Gotham will have no choice but to bow to the name Oswald Cobblepot, and give me the respect I've always richly deserved. Or I'll turn all of Gotham's birds into my own personal fowl army."

"**HAHAHAHAHA!**" He laughed again, delighted by the pigeon bullying the scientist. "Birds will be bullied by other animals and humans no longer!" he cried triumphantly. "My beautiful birds will bring Gotham City to its knees!"

Raising his umbrella, the Penguin turned off the high-frequency projectors in the sparrow's eyes.

TWEEEEEEET!

Instantly, the pigeon quit pecking at the henchman.

The pigeon landed on the scientist's shoulder, tilting its head as if nothing had happened.

The Penguin hopped down from the jeweled sparrow statue, chuckling. "Let's go get the video footage," he said, poking at the henchman with his sharp umbrella. "Get moving, Dr. Do-nothing. I want to give them a midnight deadline."

"Yes, sir," the scientist said. He helped Oswald Cobblepot back down the rungs of the ladder to the top of his office.

CHAPTER 5

FOR THE BIRDS

The second they were gone, Catwoman stepped out of the shadows. Now she had two reasons for stealing the jewels.

There was nothing Catwoman loved more than stealing something shiny and expensive. That was still her primary reason for doing the deed. But she couldn't let her home city be ruled by a crazy bird-brained villain, either.

It was already 11:30 PM. If he hadn't already, the Penguin would soon give his midnight deadline to news channels.

Catwoman had to hurry. There was no time to pick out more diamonds one by one. That wouldn't foil Penguin's scheme, anyway. She would have to use the crane to steal the entire sparrow statue.

Catwoman ran along the edge of the lower roof. In moments, she had climbed up to the operator's cab. After sliding into the seat, Catwoman activated the crane's motor. The whole cab vibrated with power. Catwoman slowly swung the crane's crossbeam over the top of the skyscraper, then pushed the lever until the trolley was directly above the sparrow statue.

CLANK! She immediately lowered the hook. Catwoman managed to snag the hook around the sparrow's neck on her first try. She pulled back on a lever, hoisting the sparrow upward.

SKREEEEEEECH! The statue violently ripped free from the top of the spire. With the sparrow statue dangling dangerously, Catwoman swung the crane's crossbeam out over the city. She began to lower the statue alongside Cobblepot Tower toward an alley below.

NOK! NOK! There came a noise from outside the crane's cab window. Batman glared at her. "Just what do you think you're doing?" he growled.

"I'm saving Gotham City," she said.

"Explain," said Batman. "Quickly."

"The Penguin has a plan," Catwoman said. "A device in the sparrow's head makes birds go cuckoo. I saw the Penguin make a pigeon attack his poor henchman. He plans to use the wild birds to hold the city hostage. And I'm stopping him."

"And stealing the jeweled statue in the process," said Batman.

"Icing on the cake," Catwoman said.

Batman's cape whipped behind him in the wind. He stared at her for a long moment, considering what to do. "Fine," he said. "I'll help you stop the Penguin. But the sparrow statue goes to the police."

Catwoman smirked. Then she continued lowering the statue toward the ground far below.

Suddenly, a door near the top of the building slammed open with a **THUD!** The Penguin stuck his head out.

"A bat and a cat are trying to steal my bird!" the Penguin cried out. He raised his umbrella. **PEW! PEW! PEW!** Sizzling energy pulses fired from its tip.

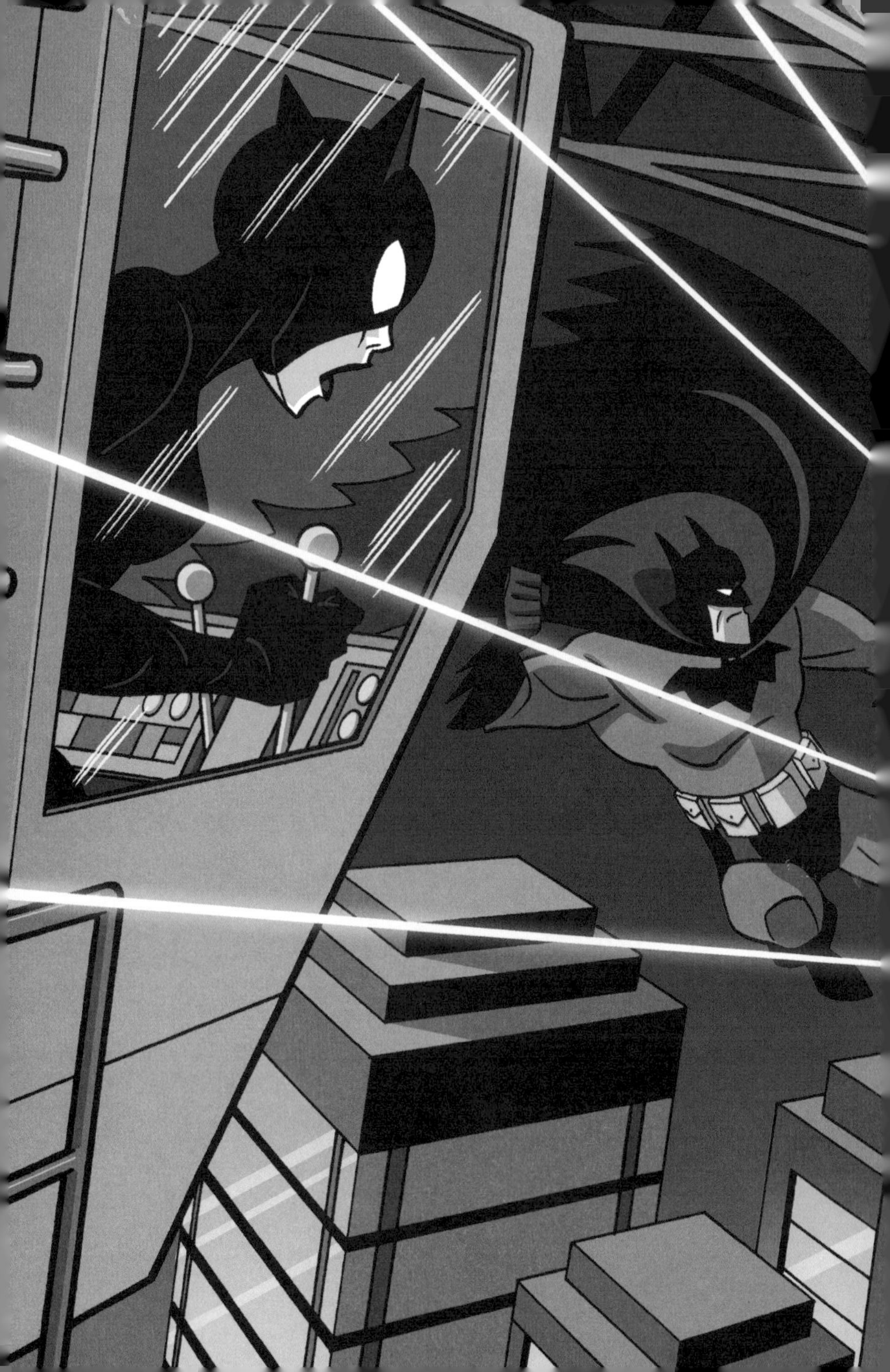

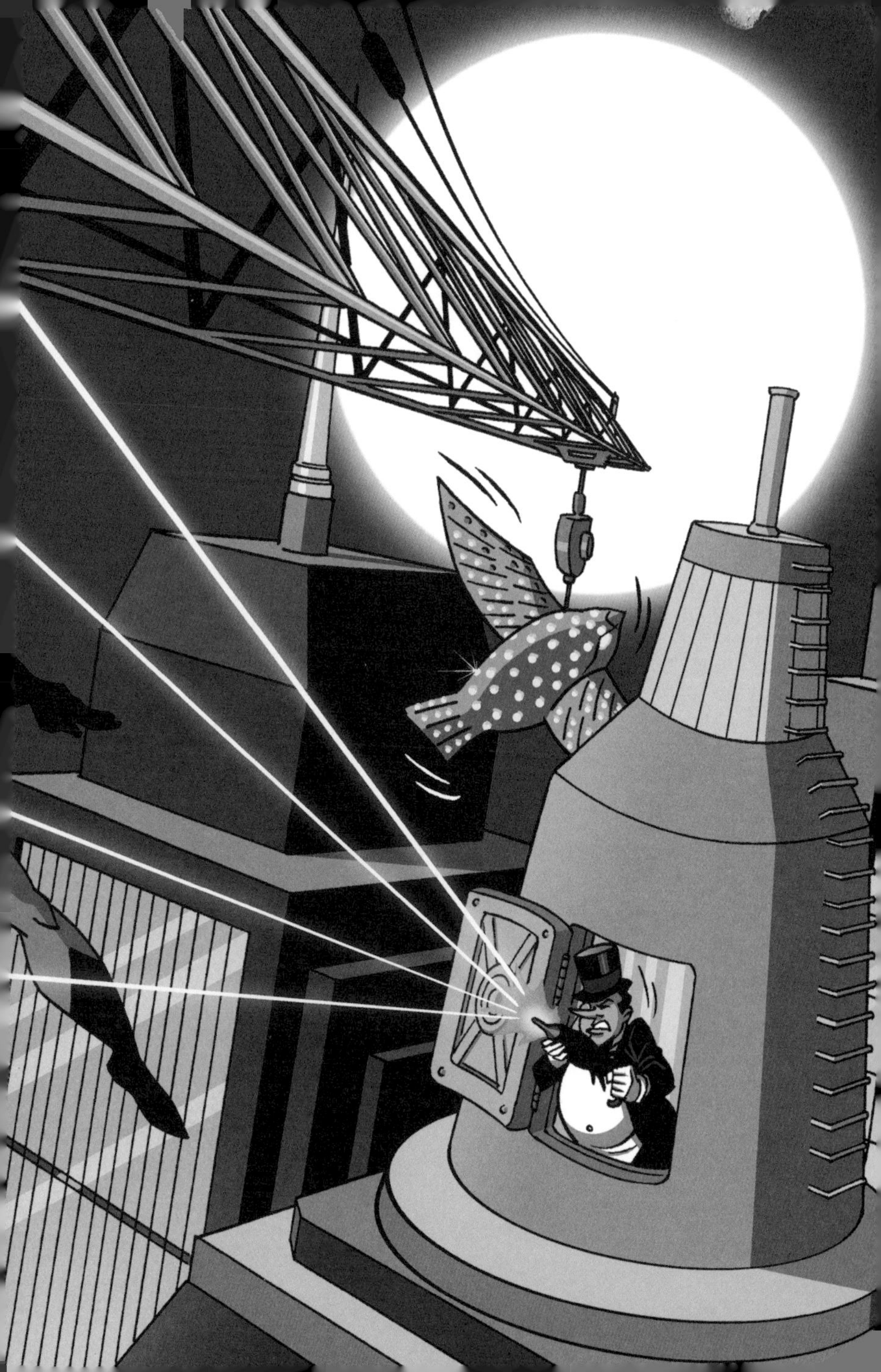

Batman sprang off the cab toward the roof. Catwoman set the crane's winch to keep lowering the sparrow statue automatically. Then she leaped out of the cab, and then landed near Batman on the roof. Batman pulled open a door at the base of the spire and rushed inside. Catwoman bounded in after him.

As soon as Catwoman and Batman came through the door, the Penguin fired a barrage of energy bolts at them from his umbrella. **PEW! PEW! PEW!**

Catwoman dived out of the way, somersaulting across the raw concrete floor.

She ducked behind a giant spool of wire while Batman took shelter behind a stack of dusty bags of cement.

"You can't hide from me!" the Penguin croaked.

He blasted his umbrella weapon at the bags of cement. **ZAP!** **FOOM!** They exploded in white clouds of power.

Batman rolled out of harm's way, ending up trapped behind the cover of a big buzzsaw.

Catwoman took a deep breath, and then zoomed out from behind the spool. **WOOOOOOOSH! ZAP!** She leaped over the energy blasts and grabbed onto the exposed steam pipes in the ceiling.

SWOOOOOOOOOOOOOSH!
The pipes broke free, spraying clouds of steam in the Penguin's face. Batman took the opportunity to tackle the Penguin, knocking him to the floor with a **THUMP!**

"You have no proof I was up to anything!" the Penguin screeched. "My lawyers will keep me out of jail forever!"

Catwoman grabbed the umbrella and ran for the roof door.

"You might go free," Batman said to the Penguin, "but I'll be watching you very carefully . . ." His voice trailed off as Catwoman snuck away.

The moment she was back outside, Catwoman leaped off the roof. She grabbed the cable connected from the crane to the sparrow statue. She slid all the way down to the alley, where the statue had landed on top of her waiting pickup truck.

Catwoman quickly disconnected the statue from the winch hook, and then flipped herself into the driver's seat. She started to drive out of the alley.

THUMP! Batman landed on the hood of Catwoman's truck.

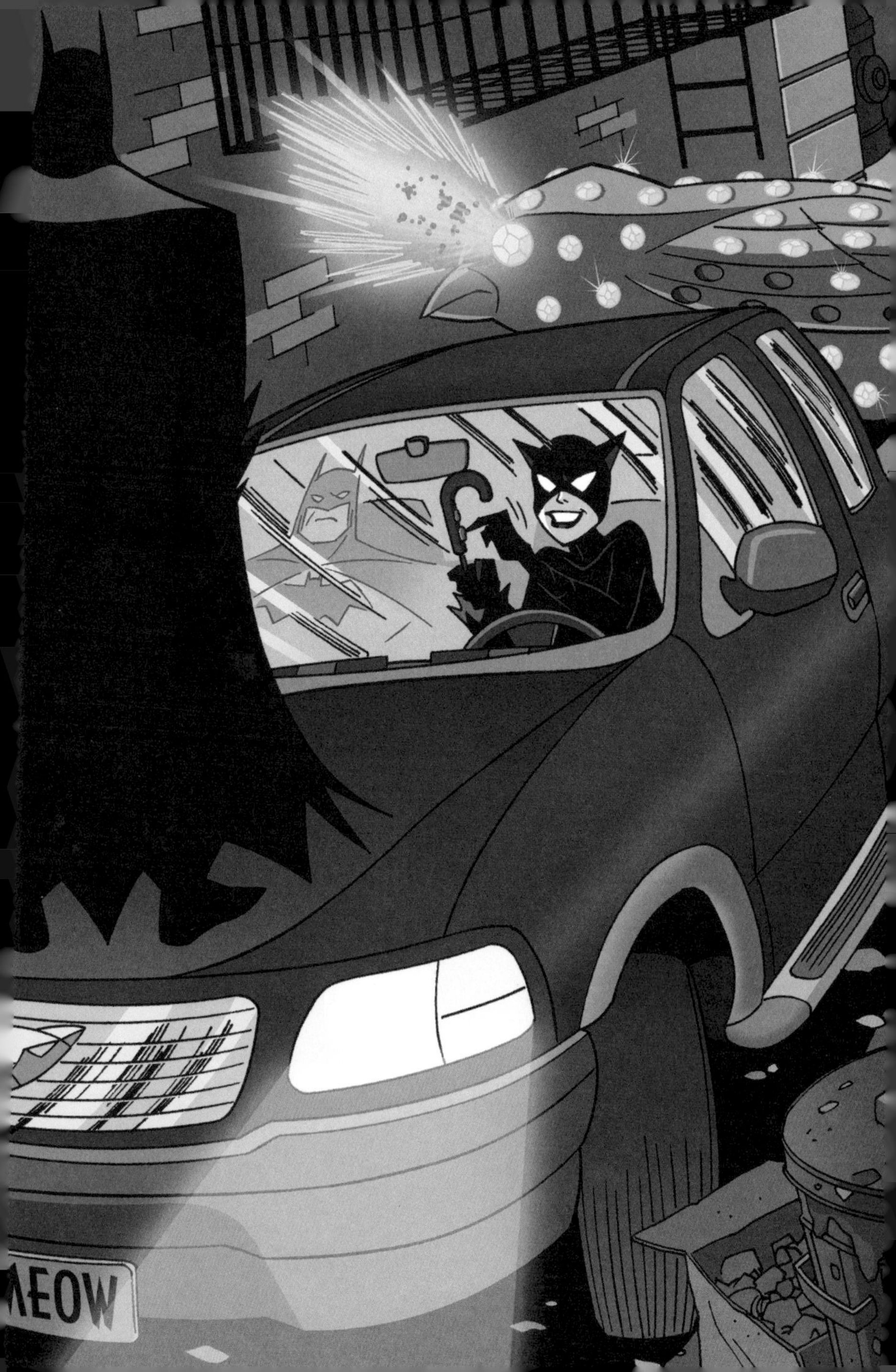

Catwoman grinned at him. She held up the Penguin's umbrella, and pressed a button on the handle. **CLICK!**

On the truck's bed, the sparrow statue's eyes glowed with ugly purplish light.

FWAP FWAP FWAP! The sound of flapping wings filled the air.

Batman glanced up and grunted as dozens of pigeons, sparrows, starlings, bluejays, and other city birds angrily attacked him. They knocked him sideways off the truck's hood.

Catwoman slammed on the gas. **SKREEEEEECH!** The truck tore out of the alley. Before she turned the corner onto the street, Catwoman glanced into her rearview mirror to see Batman shielding himself from the birds. She smiled and then zoomed away.

As soon as she'd driven the truck into a dark tunnel, Catwoman turned off the sparrow statue. Batman had only been fighting the birds a few minutes. She was sure he'd be fine.

Catwoman smiled. She was quite pleased with her escape. She'd managed to save the city . . . and steal thousands of dollars in gigantic diamonds.

Now she also had a scary weapon in her possession. Once she stripped the statue of the jewels, she'd send it secretly to the police, along with the Penguin's umbrella. Batman might overlook the theft of the diamonds, but he would hunt her down for sure if she kept such a dangerous device.

"Besides, the Penguin's plan was insane," Catwoman said to herself. "It was strictly for the birds!"

SUPER HEROES VS.

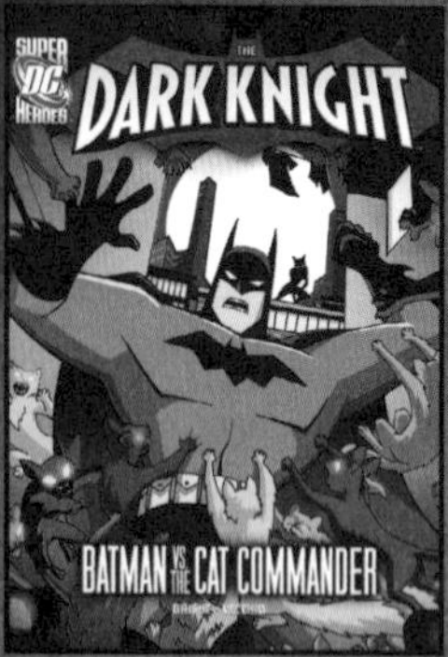
SUPER DC HEROES
THE DARK KNIGHT
BATMAN VS THE CAT COMMANDER

BATMAN VS. THE CAT COMMANDER

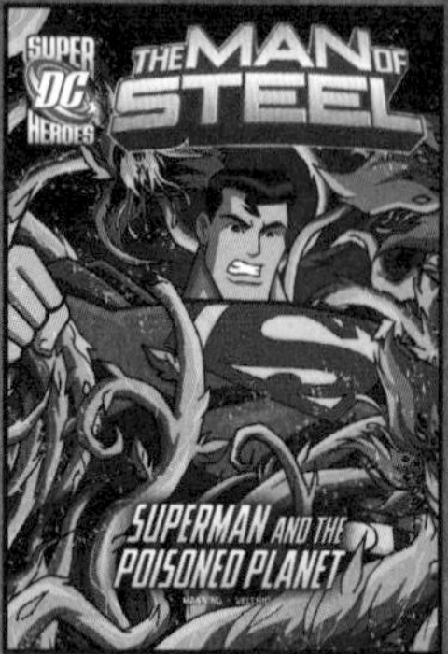
SUPER DC HEROES
THE MAN OF STEEL
SUPERMAN AND THE POISONED PLANET

SUPERMAN AND THE POISONED PLANET

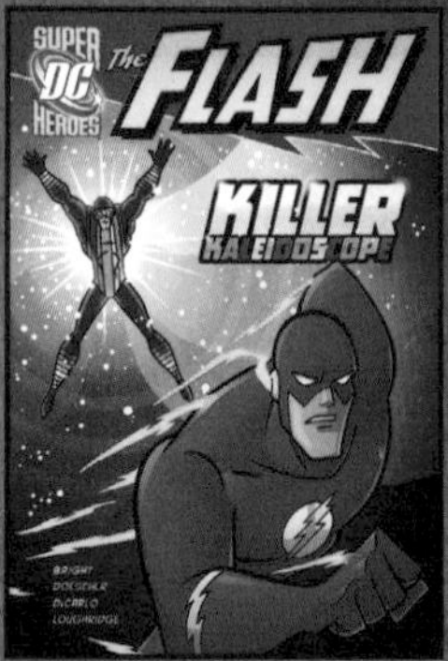
SUPER DC HEROES
The FLASH
KILLER KALEIDOSCOPE

THE FLASH: KILLER KALEIDOSCOPE

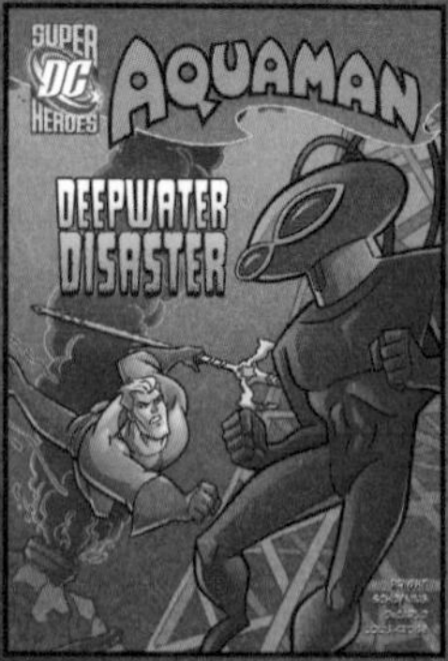
SUPER DC HEROES
AQUAMAN
DEEPWATER DISASTER

AQUAMAN: DEEPWATER DISASTER

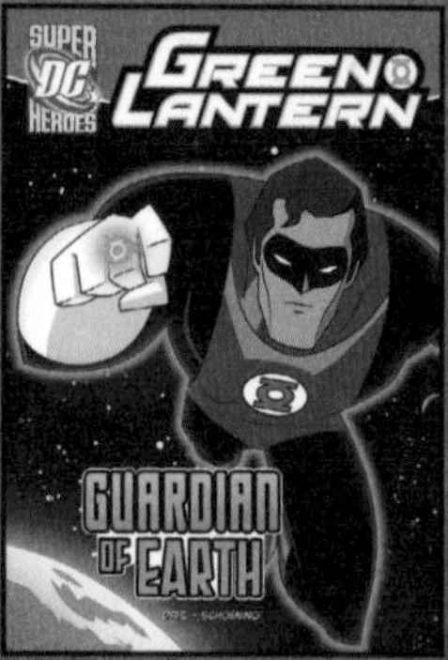
SUPER DC HEROES
GREEN LANTERN
GUARDIAN OF EARTH

GREEN LANTERN: GUARDIAN OF EARTH

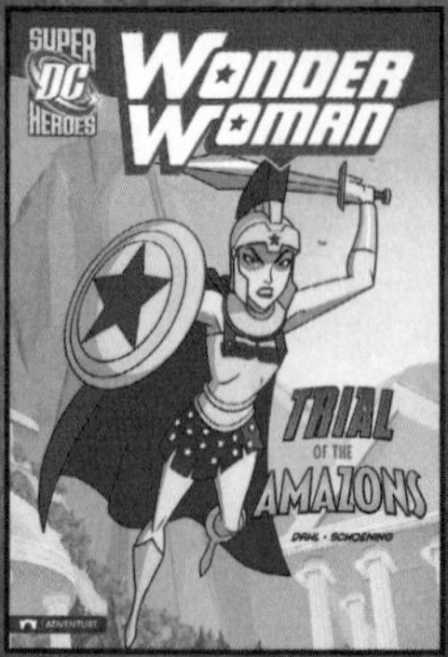
SUPER DC HEROES
WONDER WOMAN
TRIAL OF THE AMAZONS
DAHL · SCHOENING

WONDER WOMAN: TRIAL OF THE AMAZONS

WHICH SIDE...

SUPER-VILLAINS

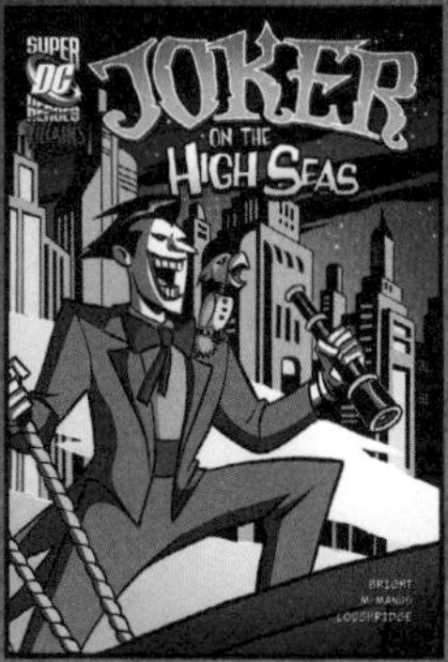
SUPER DC HEROES VILLAINS
JOKER ON THE HIGH SEAS
BRIGHT
McMANUS
LOUGHRIDGE

JOKER ON THE HIGH SEAS

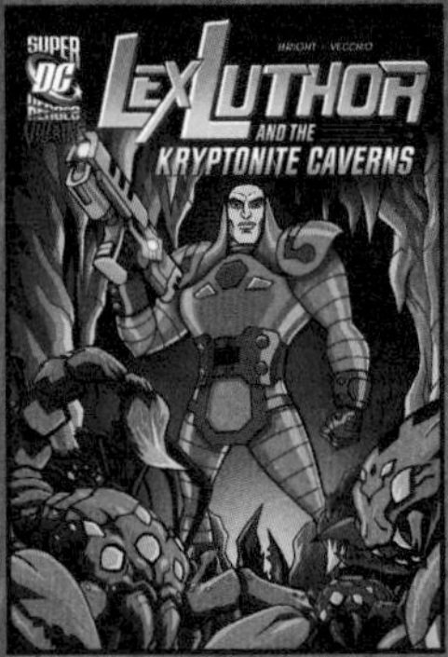
SUPER DC HEROES VILLAINS
BRIGHT · VECCHIO
LEX LUTHOR AND THE KRYPTONITE CAVERNS

LEX LUTHOR AND THE KRYPTONITE CAVERNS

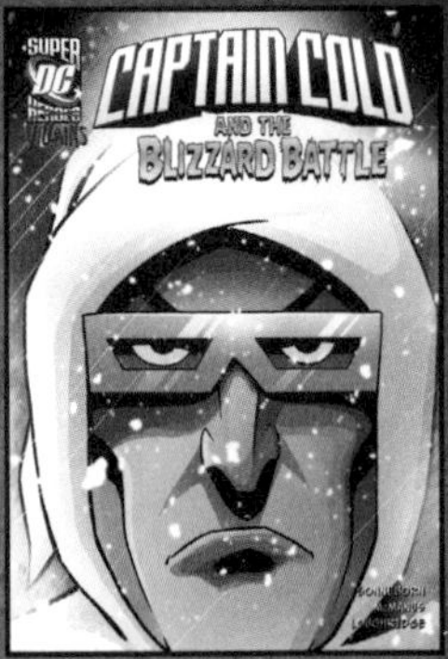
SUPER DC HEROES VILLAINS
CAPTAIN COLD AND THE BLIZZARD BATTLE

CAPTAIN COLD AND THE BLIZZARD BATTLE

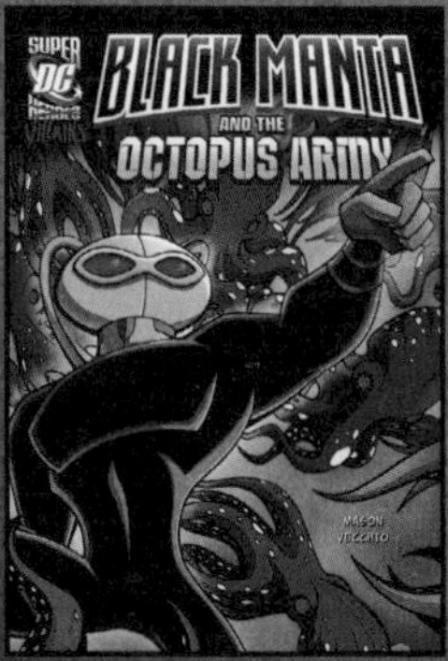
SUPER DC HEROES VILLAINS
BLACK MANTA AND THE OCTOPUS ARMY
MASON
VECCHIO

BLACK MANTA AND THE OCTOPUS ARMY

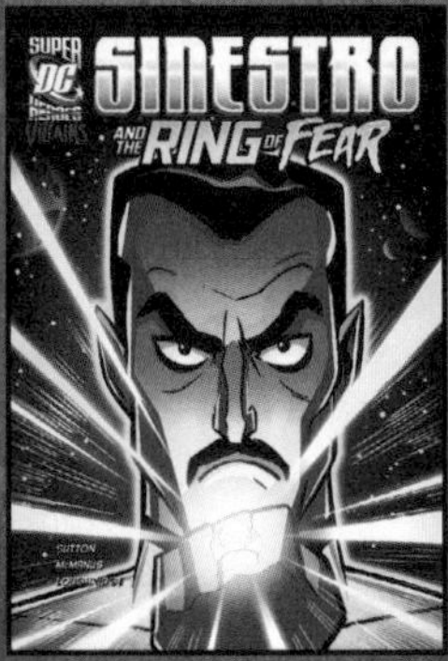
SUPER DC HEROES VILLAINS
SINESTRO AND THE RING OF FEAR
SUTTON
McMANUS

SINESTRO AND THE RING OF FEAR

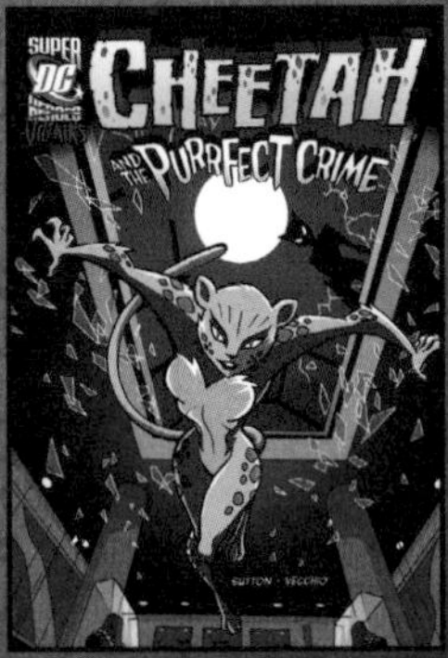
SUPER DC HEROES VILLAINS
CHEETAH AND THE PURRFECT CRIME
SUTTON · VECCHIO

CHEETAH AND THE PURRFECT CRIME

WILL YOU CHOOSE?

IF YOU WERE *BATMAN*

Batman does not have superpowers, but he's still a hero. If you were Batman, which of his techniques and tools would you use to catch crooks?

Batman chose the bat as his symbol. Why do you think he chose a bat to represent him?

IF YOU WERE CATWOMAN

Catwoman is a master thief. Based on what you know about her character, what kinds of things do you think she'd want to steal?

Who was more to blame for Batman's problems in this book — Catwoman or the Penguin? Why?

AUTHOR BIO

J.E. Bright is the author of many novels, novelizations, and novelty books for children and young adults. He lives in a sunny apartment in the Washington Heights neighborhood of Manhattan with his difficult but soft cat, Mabel, and his sweet kitten, Bernard.

SUPER HERO GLOSSARY

adversary (AD-ver-ser-ee)—someone who fights against you. Catwoman is Batman's adversary.

grapnel gun (GRAP-nuhl GUN)—Batman's grapnel gun is a cord attached to a firing mechanism that fires out and attaches to objects. It allows him to soar through the air and travel great distances very quickly.

poised (POIZD)—balanced and prepared, like Batman when he battles Catwoman atop a skyscraper

Utility Belt (yoo-TIL-uh-tee BELT)—Batman's Utility Belt contains all his crime-fighting gadgets and detective tools.

ILLUSTRATOR BIO

Tim Levins is best known for his work on the Eisner Award-winning DC Comics series, Batman: Gotham Adventures. Tim has illustrated other DC titles, such as Justice League Adventures, Batgirl, Metal Men, and Scooby Doo, and has also done work for Marvel Comics and Archie Comics. Tim enjoys life in Midland, Ontario, Canada, with his wife, son, puppy, and two horses.

SUPER-VILLAIN GLOSSARY

catsuit (KAT-soot)—a one-piece item of clothing that is form-fitting and usually black

henchman (HENCH-man)—a lackey or underling. The Penguin has many henchmen who he pays to do his bidding.

panorama (pah-nuh-RAM-uh)—a wide or complete view of an area, like the view seen from atop Cobblepot Tower

sleek (SLEEK)—smooth and shiny, like Catwoman's catsuit

ultraviolet (uhl-truh-VYE-uh-lit)—light that cannot be seen by the human eye. Catwoman has goggles that let her see ultraviolet light.

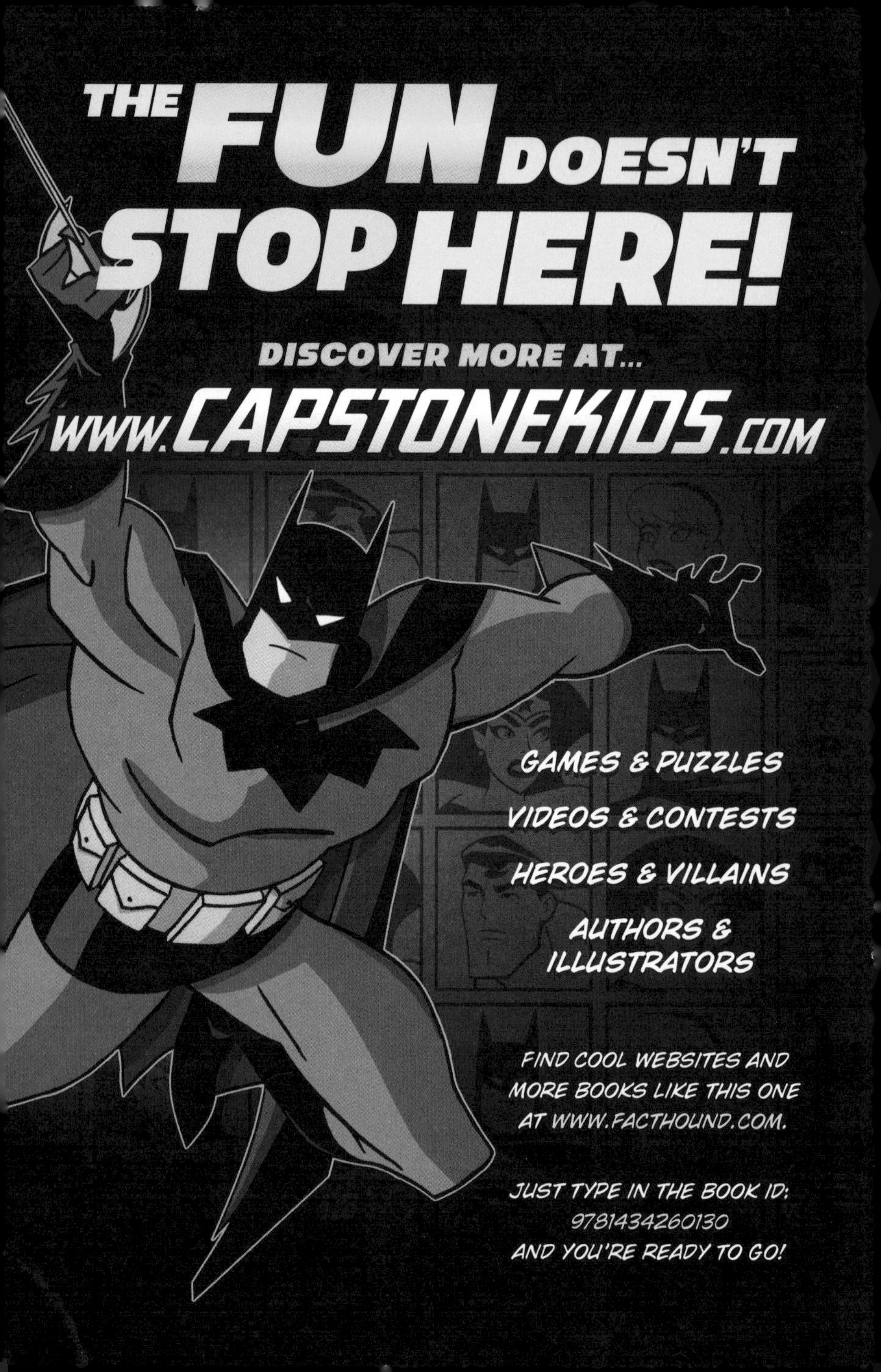
THE FUN DOESN'T STOP HERE!
DISCOVER MORE AT...
WWW.CAPSTONEKIDS.COM
GAMES & PUZZLES
VIDEOS & CONTESTS
HEROES & VILLAINS
AUTHORS & ILLUSTRATORS
FIND COOL WEBSITES AND MORE BOOKS LIKE THIS ONE AT WWW.FACTHOUND.COM.
JUST TYPE IN THE BOOK ID:
9781434260130
AND YOU'RE READY TO GO!

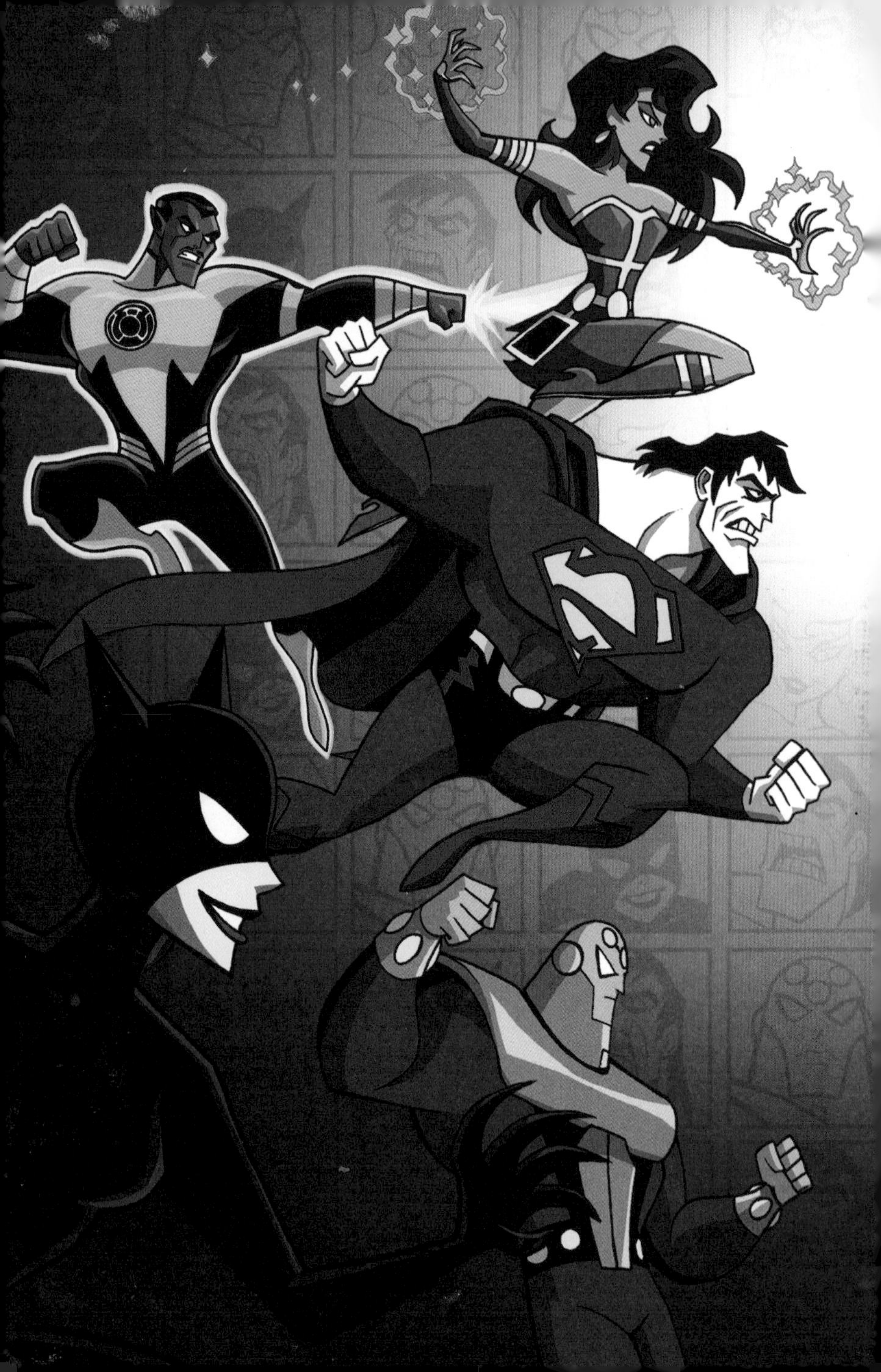